Goliath – The Boy Who Was Different
by Ximo Abadía

This book was edited and designed by gestalten
Edited by Angela Sangma Francis and Robert Klanten

Design and layout by Jan Blessing

Typeface: Super Grotesk by Arno Drescher

Printed by Grafisches Centrum Cuno GmbH & Co. KG, Calbe (Saale)
Made in Germany

Published by Little Gestalten, Berlin 2019
ISBN 978-3-89955-826-5

© Die Gestalten Verlag GmbH & Co. KG, Berlin 2019

For more information, and to order books, please visit
www.little.gestalten.com.

Bibliographic information published by the Deutsche Nationalbibliothek.
The Deutsche Nationalbibliothek lists this publication in the Deutsche
Nationalbibliografie; detailed bibliographic data are available online at
www.dnb.de.

This book was printed on paper certified according to the standards
of the FSC®.

FSC
www.fsc.org

MIX
Paper from
responsible sources
FSC® C043106

Goliath
The Boy Who Was Different

Ximo Abadía

LITTLE
GESTALTEN

Ever since I was born,
I knew I was different.

I was big.

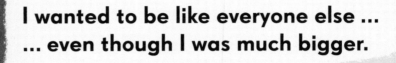

I wanted to be like everyone else ...
... even though I was much bigger.

But after a while, I began to feel like I did not belong. No one else looked like me.

I tried to do new things. "Maybe I could be a boxer?" I thought, since I was big and strong.

But no one wanted to be my opponent, because I was bigger than them.

Maybe the problem was this place? Because there was no one here who looked like me.

I had to find others who
were as big as me!

So I went to ask the ocean. It was huge and covered most of the planet, perhaps it would know where I should go?

The ocean tossed me around
in its big, salty waves and
roared loudly, but it did not
have any answers for me.

So I went to ask the sun. It was huge and ancient, it could see the whole universe. Surely the sun must know everything. Maybe it could tell me where I belonged?

The sun warmed my face with its rays, but it did not answer me. I was met with silence.

I felt small and even more lonely. I walked and walked, and it grew dark.

Was there really no one who could help me?

But then suddenly I heard a voice from high above.

The moon said, "Goliath, look at me. I am smaller than the sun, and I am bigger than the ocean, but it does not matter, because there is no one else like me. So, why does it matter to you if you are big or small?"

I thought long and hard.

And then I realized, the moon
was right. It made no difference
at all, if I was big or small!

Whoever was looking at me ...

... would never see me in the same way.

At last I understood.
I didn't need to find
others as big as me.

There was no one like me!
And I belonged here, exactly
the way I was.

We are all different and
no matter what we look like,
we are all special.

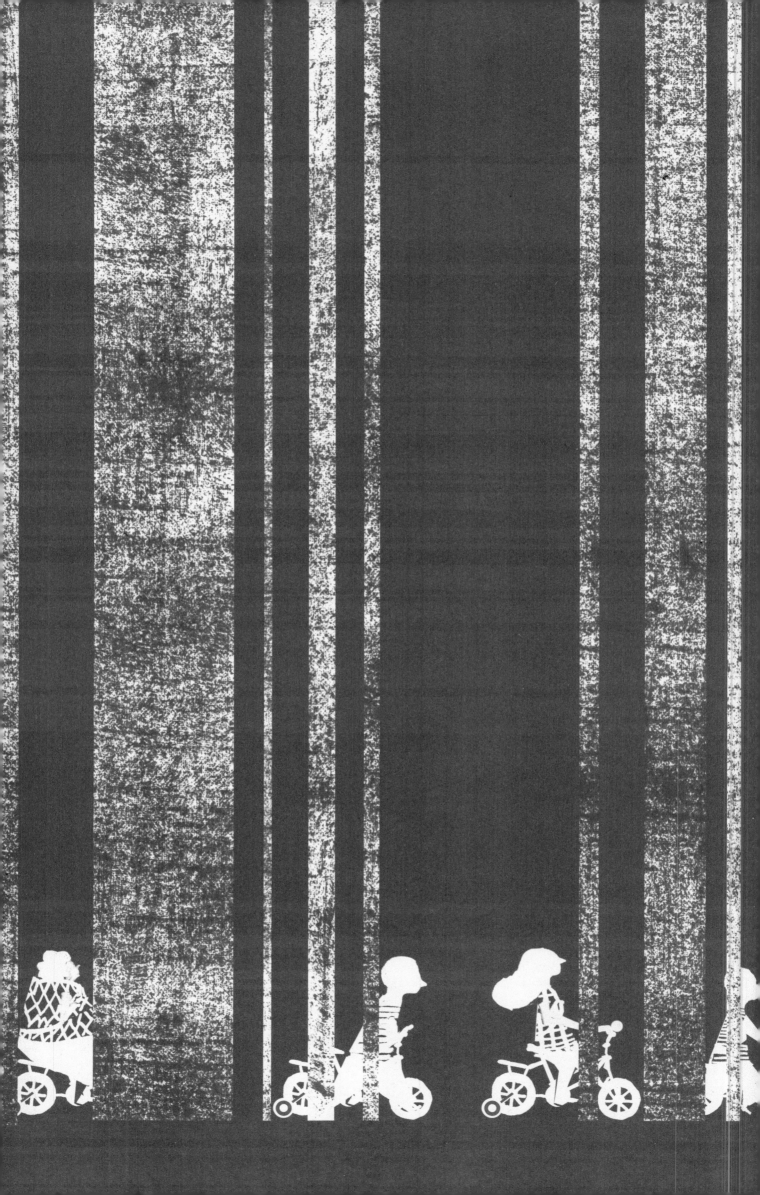